BUFFALO BILLS

BY JOSH ANDERSON

Stride
An Imprint of The Child's World®
childsworld.com

The Child's World
childsworld.com

Published by The Child's World®
800-599-READ • www.childsworld.com

Photography Credits
Cover: © Timothy T Ludwig / Stringer / Getty Images; page 1: © Africa Studio / Shutterstock; page 3: © Maria Lysaker/ZUMA Press / Newscom; page 5: © Justin K. Aller / Stringer / Getty Images; page 6: © George Rose / Stringer / Getty Images; page 9: © Maddie Malhotra / Stringer / Getty Images; page 10: © Brett Carlsen / Stringer / Getty Images; page 11: © stevezmina1 / Getty Images; page 12: © Bryan M. Bennett / Stringer / Getty Images; page 12: © Jonathan Daniel / Staff / Getty Images; page 13: © Brett Carlsen / Stringer / Getty Images; page 13: © Timothy T Ludwig / Stringer / Getty Images; page 14: © Brett Carlsen / Stringer / Getty Images; page 15: © Rick Stewart / Stringer / Getty Images; page 16: © Rick Stewart / Stringer / Getty Images; page 16: © Rick Stewart / Stringer / Getty Images; page 17: © Simon Bruty / Staff / Getty Images; page 17: © Rick Stewart / Stringer / Getty Images; page 18: © Rick Stewart / Stringer / Getty Images; page 18: © Rick Stewart / Stringer / Getty Images; page 19: © Tom Pennington / Staff / Getty Images; page 19: © Bryan M. Bennett / Stringer / Getty Images; page 20: © Maddie Meyer / Staff / Getty Images; page 20: © Timothy T Ludwig / Stringer / Getty Images; page 21: © Michael Reaves / Stringer / Getty Images; page 21: © Harry How / Staff / Getty Images; page 22: © Rick Stewart / Stringer / Getty Images; page 23: © Andy Lyons / Staff / Getty Images; page 23: © stevezmina1 / Getty Images; page 25: © Rick Stewart / Stringer / Getty Images; page 26: © Rick Stewart / Stringer / Getty Images; page 29: © Rick Stewart / Stringer / Getty Images

ISBN Information
9781503857742 (Reinforced Library Binding)
9781503860414 (Portable Document Format)
9781503861770 (Online Multi-user eBook)
9781503863132 (Electronic Publication)

LCCN 2021952620

Printed in the United States of America

BRINGING THE WORLD TO YOUNG READERS 1968

TABLE OF CONTENTS

GO BILLS!

The Buffalo Bills compete in the National Football **League's** (NFL's) American Football Conference (AFC). They play in the AFC East **division**, along with the New York Jets, Miami Dolphins, and New England Patriots. The Bills are one of Buffalo's two professional sports teams. The team once played in four straight **Super Bowls**. That accomplishment has never been matched by another NFL team. Let's learn more about the Bills!

AFC EAST DIVISION

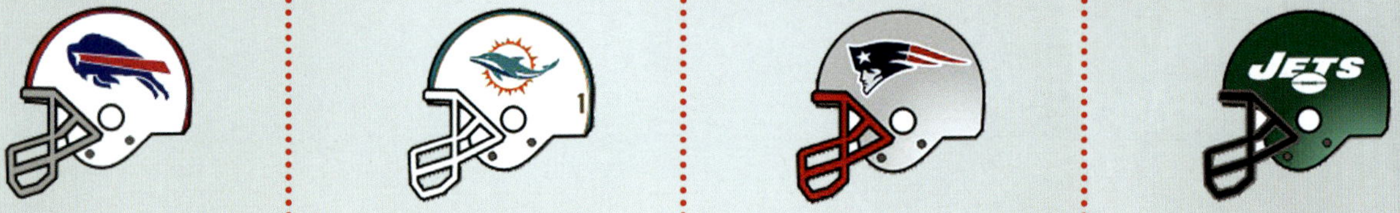

Buffalo Bills	Miami Dolphins	New England Patriots	New York Jets

IN 2020, THE BILLS CELEBRATED THEIR FIRST AFC EAST DIVISION TITLE SINCE 1995.

BECOMING THE BILLS

The city of Buffalo has been home to a few professional football teams since 1920. The Buffalo All Americans, the Bisons, and the Tigers set the stage for the team that eventually became the Buffalo Bills. The Bills began play in 1960 as an original member of the American Football League (AFL). During their time in the AFL, the Bills won two AFL Championships. They joined the NFL in 1970 when the AFL and NFL merged to form one league. The team is named after William "Buffalo Bill" Cody, a hero of the Old West.

JOE FERGUSON (RIGHT) LED THE BILLS TO 77 WINS AS THE TEAM'S QUARTERBACK FROM 1973 TO 1984.

BY THE NUMBERS

The Bills have played in **FOUR** Super Bowls.

NINE
AFC East division titles for the Bills

501
points scored by the team in 2020—a Bills record!

TWO
AFL Championships for the Bills

DEVIN SINGLETARY EARNED THE NICKNAME "MOTOR" AS A PLAYER AT FLORIDA ATLANTIC UNIVERSITY BECAUSE HE NEVER SLOWS DOWN.

OUTDOOR COOKOUTS, KNOWN AS TAILGATING, ARE A HUGE TRADITION OUTSIDE OF HIGHMARK STADIUM BEFORE BILLS GAMES.

GAME DAY

The Bills play their home games in Buffalo, New York. Because the New York Jets and Giants actually play in New Jersey, the Bills are the only NFL team actually based in New York State. Highmark **Stadium** has been home to the Bills since 1973. The stadium holds about 72,000 fans. Because Buffalo is so far north, fans and players often face chilly temperatures during the wintertime. But the cold doesn't stop fans in Buffalo from coming out to root on the Bills!

We're Famous!

In 1998, popular Bills quarterback Doug Flutie wanted to help raise money for the Doug Flutie Jr. Foundation for Autism. His son is autistic, so the cause was close to Flutie's heart. He partnered with a food company to create a breakfast cereal called Flutie Flakes. The company produced 50,000 boxes at first. But Flutie Flakes were so popular, they eventually sold more than 2 million boxes!

UNIFORM

Truly Weird

Playing football in snowy conditions isn't that weird. But during a game between the Bills and Colts in 2017, nine inches (23 cm) of snow fell during the game. Only 18 passes were completed in the harsh conditions. The game was tied 7–7 and went into **overtime**. Running back LeSean McCoy scored a 21- yard rushing **touchdown** to seal a 13–7 Bills victory.

Alternate Jersey

Sometimes teams wear an alternate jersey that is different from their home and away jerseys. It might be a bright color or have a unique theme. The Bills wore these all-red uniforms for a 2020 game against the Pittsburgh Steelers. Wearing their "Color Rush" uniforms, the Bills won the game 26–15.

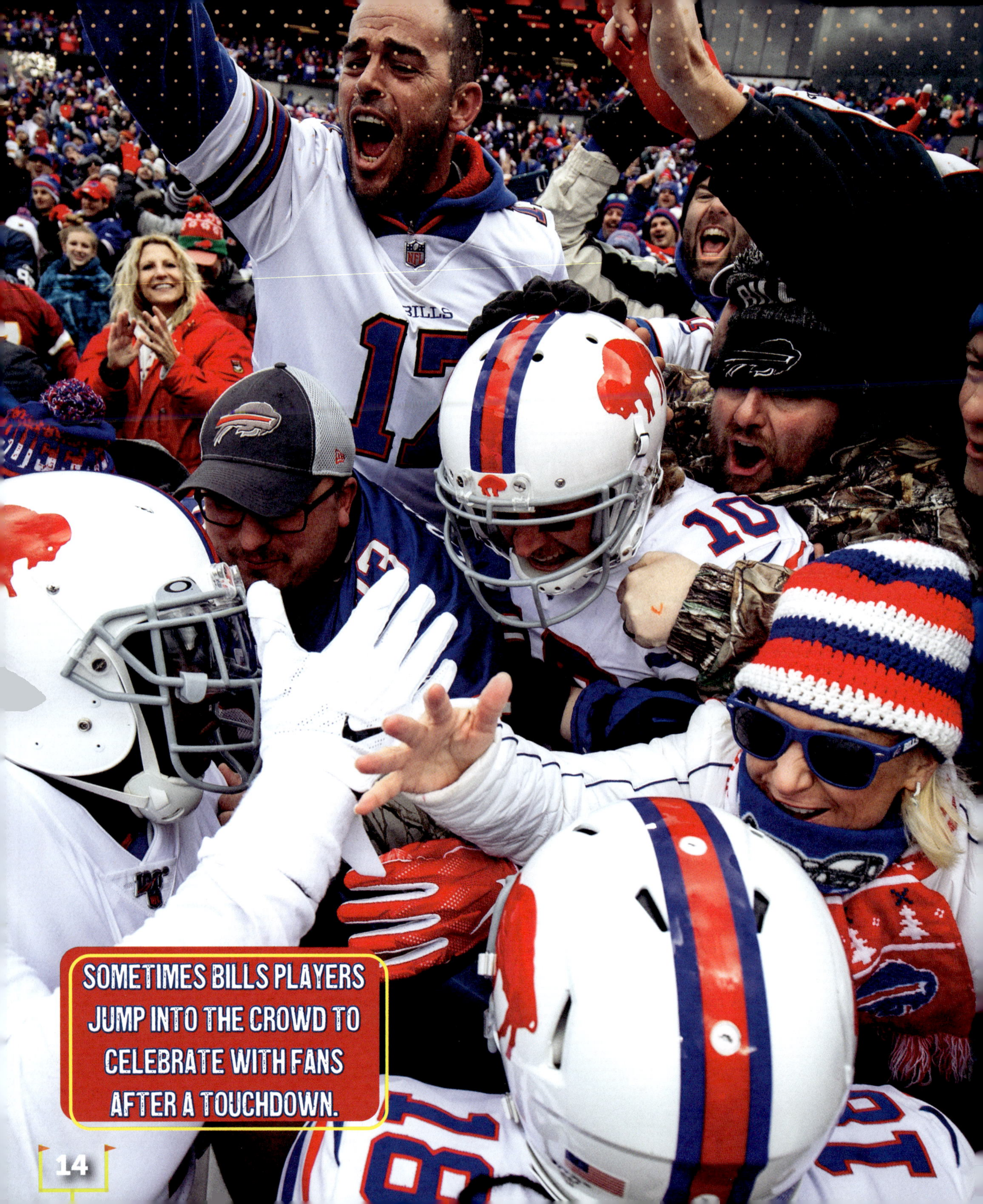

SOMETIMES BILLS PLAYERS JUMP INTO THE CROWD TO CELEBRATE WITH FANS AFTER A TOUCHDOWN.

TEAM SPIRIT

The experience of going to a Bills game at Highmark Stadium begins before fans even get to their seats. Thousands of Bills fans hold a tailgating party before every Bills game in the stadium parking lot. They enjoy food cooked on portable grills and time with friends. Inside the stadium, fans enjoy the antics of the team mascot. Billy Buffalo is a nearly-eight-foot-tall (2.4 m) blue American bison! Although the Bills do not have a cheerleading squad to support them, the Stampede Drumline plays at every Bills home game. Fans get to enjoy their music after every great play!

BILLY BUFFALO

HEROES OF HISTORY

Cornelius Bennett

Linebacker | 1987–1995

Bennett was a key part of the Bills defense during their run to four straight Super Bowls in the early 1990s. He had 52.5 **sacks** in his Bills career, and he once had four in a single game. Bennett was chosen for the **Pro Bowl** five times

Jim Kelly

Quarterback | 1986–1996

Kelly is the Bills all-time leader in passing yards (35,467) and touchdowns (237). During his 11 seasons as the Bills starting quarterback, he led the team to 101 victories and four Super Bowl appearances. Kelly was inducted into the Pro Football **Hall of Fame** in 2002.

Andre Reed

Wide Receiver | 1985–1999

Reed's 87 career receiving touchdowns rank 14th in NFL history. Reed led the Bills in receiving during nine of his seasons with the team, and he finished his career with 13,198 yards. The seven-time Pro Bowler was elected to the Pro Football Hall of Fame in 2014.

Thurman Thomas

Running Back | 1988–1999

The winner of the 1991 **Most Valuable Player** (MVP) Award, Thomas led the Bills in rushing for nine straight seasons. He finished his career with 65 rushing touchdowns and 12,074 yards. He was chosen for the Pro Bowl five times and was inducted into the Pro Football Hall of Fame in 2007.

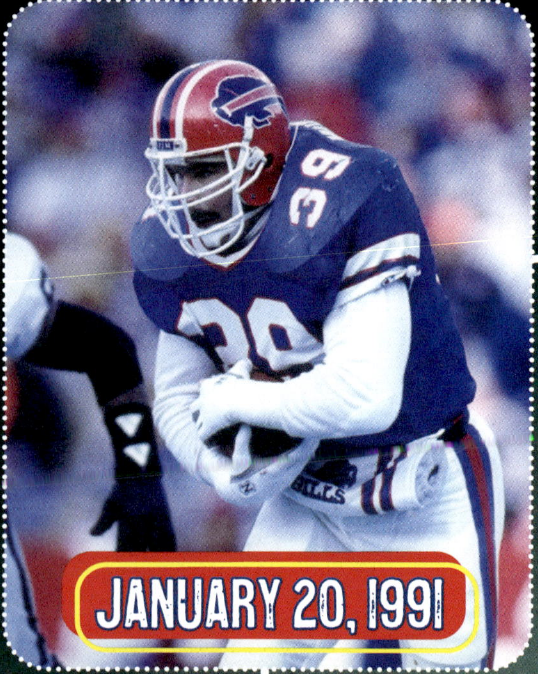

In one of the biggest blowouts in playoff history, the Bills defeat the Los Angeles Raiders 51–3. The win takes the Bills to their first Super Bowl.

Thurman Thomas rushes for three touchdowns in the AFC Championship Game. The Bills defeat the Kansas City Chiefs 30–13 and advance to their fourth straight Super Bowl.

BIG DAYS

The Bills draft quarterback Josh Allen with the seventh pick in the first round of the NFL Draft. Allen becomes the team's starting quarterback early in his **rookie** year.

The Bills defeat the Baltimore Ravens 17–3 to advance to the AFC Championship Game for the first time since 1993.

MODERN-DAY MARVELS

Josh Allen

Quarterback | Debut: 2018

In 2020, Allen became the first player in NFL history to compile at least 4,000 passing yards, 30 passing touchdowns, and eight rushing touchdowns in the same season. He was selected for the Pro Bowl for his accomplishment and finished second in MVP voting.

Stefon Diggs

Wide Receiver | Debut: 2020

After five seasons with the Minnesota Vikings, Diggs joined the Bills in 2020. In his first season with the team, he led the NFL with 127 catches and 1,535 receiving yards. The sure-handed Diggs was chosen for the Pro Bowl after the 2020 and 2021 seasons.

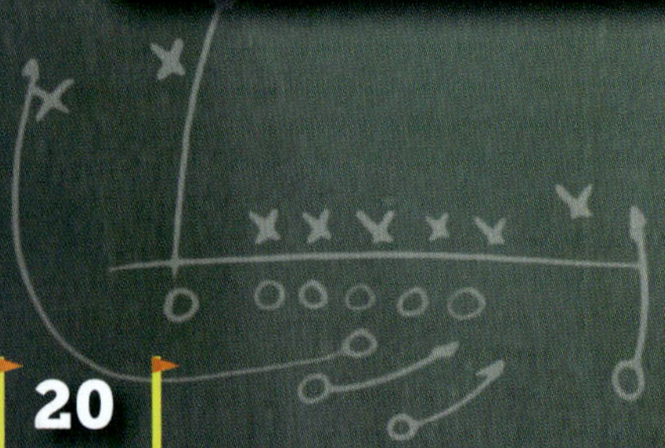

Tremaine Edmunds

Linebacker | Debut: 2018

Edmunds became the first player in NFL history to have two seasons with more than 100 tackles by the time he was 21 years old. In 2018, the two-time Pro Bowler also became the youngest player in NFL history to intercept a pass.

Tre'Davious White

Cornerback | Debut: 2017

After he played at Louisiana State University, the Bills made White a first-round draft pick in 2017. A two-time Pro Bowler, he's one of the toughest pass defenders in the league. In 2019, White tied for the league lead with six interceptions.

DEFENSIVE LINEMAN BRUCE SMITH WAS CHOSEN AS THE NFL'S DEFENSIVE PLAYER OF THE YEAR TWICE.

THE GOAT

GREATEST OF ALL TIME

BRUCE SMITH

An almost unstoppable force on the defensive line, Smith is the NFL's career leader in sacks with 200. In 15 seasons with the Bills, Smith was chosen for 11 Pro Bowls. His 43 forced fumbles are the eighth most in NFL history. Smith ranks seventh all-time with 267 games started in his career. The Hall of Famer helped lead the Bills to the Super Bowl four times.

FAN FAVORITE

Doug Flutie–Quarterback
1998–2000

After eight seasons in the Canadian Football League, Flutie became a fan favorite during his three seasons in Buffalo. He led the team to the **playoffs** in 1998 and 1999. After his football career ended, Flutie remained popular, wrestling in the WWE and appearing on *Dancing with the Stars*.

THE BIG GAME

JANUARY 3, 1993 – AFC WILD CARD GAME

In 1992, the Bills earned a trip to the playoffs as a Wild Card team. Their opponent was the Houston Oilers. The Oilers thumped the Bills in the first half to take a 28–3 lead. Then, on the Bills' first possession of the third quarter, Oiler Bubba McDowell returned an interception 58 yards for a touchdown, making the score 35–3. But the Bills scored touchdowns on their next four possessions, cutting Houston's lead to 35–31. Miraculously, the Bills took the lead in the fourth quarter and won the game 41–38 in overtime. The 32-point comeback is the greatest in NFL history.

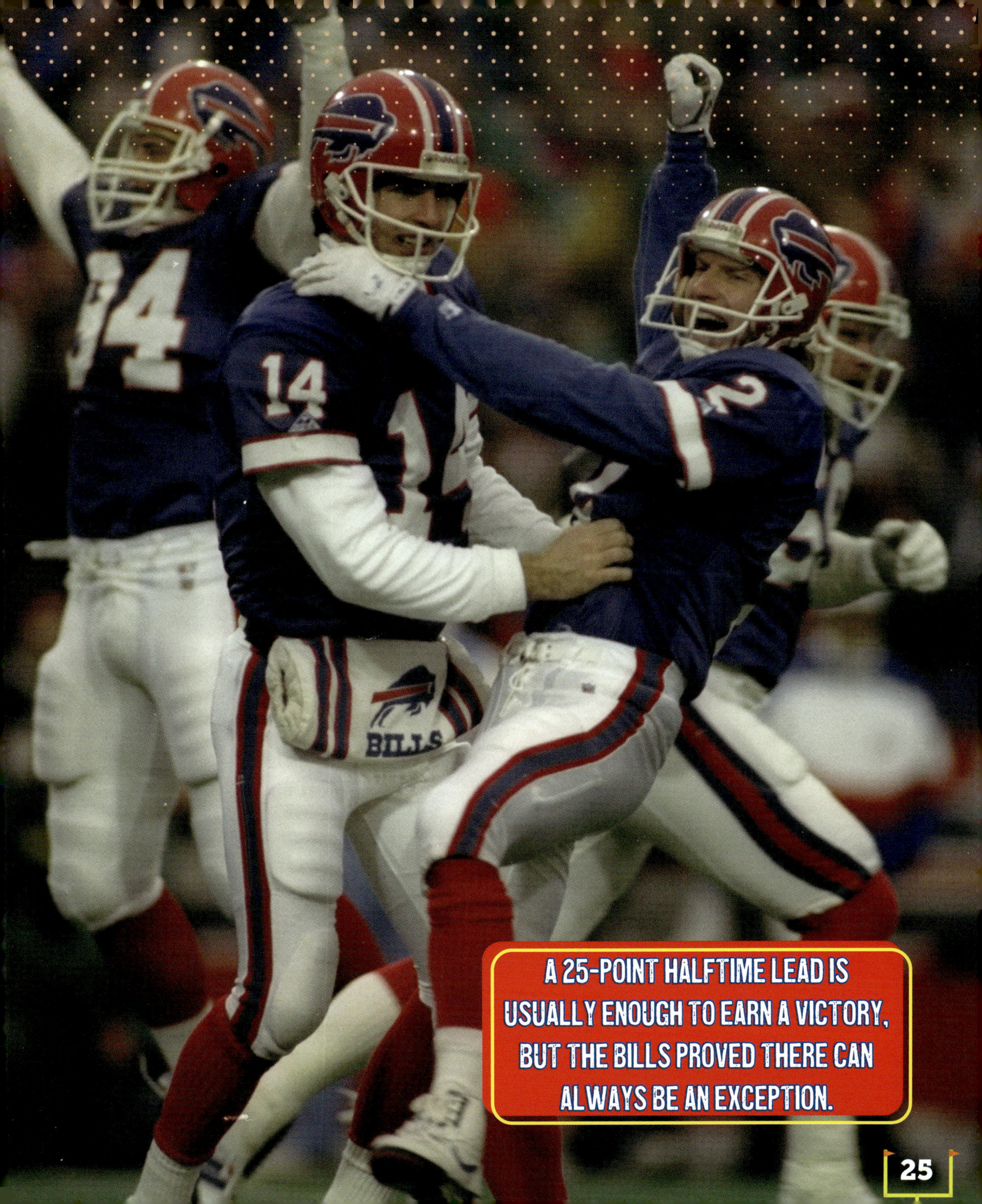

A 25-POINT HALFTIME LEAD IS USUALLY ENOUGH TO EARN A VICTORY, BUT THE BILLS PROVED THERE CAN ALWAYS BE AN EXCEPTION.

MARV LEVY LED THE BILLS TO 112 REGULAR-SEASON VICTORIES AND FOUR SUPER BOWLS.

AMAZING FEATS

237 Touchdown Passes

Thrown by QUARTERBACK Jim Kelly

86 Receiving Touchdowns

By WIDE RECEIVER Andre Reed

2,002 Rushing Yards

In 1973 by RUNNING BACK O. J. Simpson

265 Single Game Receiving Yards

In 2006 by WIDE RECEIVER Lee Evans

ALL-TIME BEST

PASSING YARDS

Jim Kelly
35,467

Joe Ferguson
27,590

Jack Kemp
15,134

RUSHING YARDS

Thurman Thomas
11,938

O. J. Simpson
10,183

Fred Jackson
5,646

RECEIVING YARDS

Andre Reed
13,095

Eric Moulds
9,096

Lee Evans
5,934

SACKS*

Bruce Smith
171

Aaron Schobel
78

Phil Hansen
61.5

SCORING

Steve Christie
1,011

Rian Lindell
980

Scott Norwood
670

INTERCEPTIONS

Butch Byrd
40

Tony Greene
37

Mark Kelso
30

*unofficial before 1982

WIDE RECEIVER ERIC MOULDS SCORED 48 TOUCHDOWNS DURING HIS TEN SEASONS WITH THE BILLS.

GLOSSARY

division (dih-VIZSH-un): a group of teams within the NFL who play each other more frequently and compete for the best record

Hall of Fame (HAHL of FAYM): a museum in Canton, Ohio, that honors the best players in NFL history.

league (LEEG): an organization of sports teams that compete against each other

Most Valuable Player (MOHST VAL-yuh-bul PLAY-uhr): a yearly award given to the top player in the NFL

overtime (OH-vuhr-tym): extra time that is played when teams are tied at the end of four quarters

playoffs (PLAY-ahfs): a series of games after the regular season that decides which two teams play in the Super Bowl

Pro Bowl (PRO BOWL): the NFL's All-Star game where the best players in the league compete

rookie (RUH-kee): a player playing in his first season

sack (SAK): when a quarterback is tackled behind the line of scrimmage before he can throw the ball

stadium (STAY-dee-uhm): a building with a field and seats for fans where teams play

Super Bowl (SOO-puhr BOWL): the championship game of the NFL, played between the winners of the AFC and the NFC

touchdown (TUTCH-down): a play in which the ball is brought into the other team's end zone, resulting in six points

FIND OUT MORE

IN THE LIBRARY

Bulgar, Beth and Mark Bechtel. *My First Book of Football.* New York, NY: Time Inc. Books, 2015.

Jacobs, Greg. *The Everything Kids' Football Book, 7th Edition*. Avon, MA: Adams Media, 2021.

Sports Illustrated Kids. *The Greatest Football Teams of All Time*. New York, NY: Time Inc. Books, 2018.

Wyner, Zach. *Buffalo Bills*. New York, NY: AV2, 2020.

ON THE WEB

Visit our website for links about the Buffalo Bills:
childsworld.com/links

Note to parents, teachers, and librarians: We routinely verify our web links to make sure they are safe and active sites. Encourage your readers to check them out!

INDEX

ABOUT THE AUTHOR

Josh Anderson has published over 50 books for children and young adults. His two boys are the greatest joys in his life. Hobbies include coaching his sons in youth basketball, no-holds-barred games of Apples to Apples, and taking long family walks. His favorite NFL team is a secret he'll never share!